THE PARSON'S DAUGHTER OF OXNEY COLNE

ANTHONY TROLLOPE

ANOTHER LEAF PRESS

```
         *
        ***
      ******
       ***
         *


         *
        ***
      *******
    **********
     ******
       ***
         *


         *
        ***
      ******
       ***
         *
```

ANOTHER LEAF PRESS

2013

THE PARSON'S DAUGHTER OF OXNEY COLNE

The prettiest scenery in all England—and if I am contradicted in that assertion, I will say in all Europe—is in Devonshire, on the southern and south-eastern skirts of Dartmoor, where the rivers Dart, and Avon, and Teign form themselves, and where the broken moor is half cultivated, and the wild-looking upland fields are half moor. In making this assertion I am often met with much doubt, but it is by persons who do not really know the locality. Men and women talk to me on the matter, who have travelled down the line of railway from Exeter to Plymouth, who have spent a fortnight at Torquay, and perhaps made an excursion from Tavistock to the convict prison on Dartmoor. But who knows the glories of Chagford? Who has walked through the parish of Manaton? Who is conversant with Lustleigh Cleeves and

Withycombe in the moor? Who has explored Holne Chase? Gentle reader, believe me that you will be rash in contradicting me, unless you have done these things.

There or thereabouts—I will not say by the waters of which little river it is washed—is the parish of Oxney Colne. And for those who wish to see all the beauties of this lovely country, a sojourn in Oxney Colne would be most desirable, seeing that the sojourner would then be brought nearer to all that he would wish to visit, than at any other spot in the country. But there in an objection to any such arrangement. There are only two decent houses in the whole parish, and these are—or were when I knew the locality—small and fully occupied by their possessors. The larger and better is the parsonage, in which lived the parson and his daughter; and the smaller is a freehold residence of a certain Miss Le Smyrger, who owned a farm of a hundred acres, which was rented by one Farmer Cloysey, and who also possessed some thirty acres round her own house, which she managed herself; regarding herself to be quite as great in cream as Mr.

Cloysey, and altogether superior to him in the article of cyder. "But yeu has to pay no rent, Miss," Farmer Cloysey would say, when Miss Le Smyrger expressed this opinion of her art in a manner too defiant. "Yeu pays no rent, or yeu couldn't do it." Miss Le Smyrger was an old maid, with a pedigree and blood of her own, a hundred and thirty acres of fee- simple land on the borders of Dartmoor, fifty years of age, a constitution of iron, and an opinion of her own on every subject under the sun.

And now for the parson and his daughter. The parson's name was Woolsworthy—or Woolathy, as it was pronounced by all those who lived around him—the Rev. Saul Woolsworthy; and his daughter was Patience Woolsworthy, or Miss Patty, as she was known to the Devonshire world of those parts. That name of Patience had not been well chosen for her, for she was a hot-tempered damsel, warm in her convictions, and inclined to express them freely. She had but two closely intimate friends in the world, and by both of them this freedom of expression had now been fully permitted to her since she was a child. Miss Le Smyrger and her father were well accustomed to her ways, and on the whole well satisfied with them. The former was equally free and equally warm-tempered as herself, and as Mr. Woolsworthy was allowed by his daughter to be quite paramount on his own subject—for he had a subject—he did not object to his daughter being paramount on all others. A pretty girl was Patience Woolsworthy at the time of which I am writing, and one who possessed much that was worthy of remark and admiration, had she lived where beauty meets with admiration, or where force of character is remarked. But at Oxney Colne, on the borders of Dartmoor, there were few to appreciate her, and it seemed as though she herself had but little idea of carrying her talent further afield, so that it might not remain for ever wrapped in a blanket.

She was a pretty girl, tall end slender, with dark eyes and black hair. Her eyes were perhaps too round for regular beauty, and her hair was perhaps too crisp; her mouth was large and expressive; her nose was finely formed, though a critic in female form might have declared it to be somewhat broad. But her countenance altogether was wonderfully attractive—if only it might be seen without that resolution for dominion which occasionally marred it, though sometimes it even added to her attractions.

It must be confessed on behalf of Patience Woolsworthy, that the circumstances of her life had peremptorily called upon her to exercise dominion. She had lost her mother when she was sixteen, and had had neither brother nor sister. She had no neighbours near her fit either from education or rank to interfere in the conduct of her life, excepting always Miss La Smyrger. Miss Le Smyrger would have done anything for her, including the whole management of her morals and of the parsonage household, had Patience been content with such an arrangement. But much as Patience had ever loved Miss Le Smyrger, she was not content with this, and therefore she had been called on to put forth a strong hand of her own. She had put forth this strong hand early, and hence had come the character which I am attempting to describe. But I must say on behalf of this girl, that it was not only over others that she thus exercised dominion. In acquiring that power she had also acquired the much greater power of exercising rule over herself.

But why should her father have been ignored in these family arrangements? Perhaps it may almost suffice to say, that of all living men her father was the man best conversant with the antiquities of the county in which he lived. He was the Jonathan Oldbuck of Devonshire, and especially of Dartmoor, without that decision of character which enabled Oldbuck to keep his womenkind in some kind of subjection, and probably enabled him also to see that his weekly bills did not pass their proper limits. Our Mr. Oldbuck, of Oxney Colne, was sadly deficient in these. As a parish pastor with but a small cure, he did his duty with sufficient energy, to keep him, at any rate, from reproach. He was kind and charitable to the poor, punctual in his services, forbearing with the farmers around him, mild with his brother clergymen, and indifferent to aught that bishop or archdeacon might think or say of him. I do not name this latter attribute as a virtue, but as a fact. But all these points were as nothing in the known character of Mr. Woolsworthy, of Oxney Colne. He was the antiquarian of Dartmoor. That was his line of life. It was in that capacity that he was known to the Devonshire world; it was as such that he journeyed about with his humble carpet-bag, staying away from his parsonage a night or two at a time; it was in that character that he received now and again stray visitors in the single spare bedroom —not friends asked to see him and his girl because of their friendship—but men who knew something as to this buried stone, or that old land-mark. In all these things his daughter let him have his own way, assisting and encouraging him. That was his line of life, and therefore she respected it. But in all other matters she chose to be paramount at the parsonage.

Mr. Woolsworthy was a little man, who always wore,

except on Sundays, grey clothes—clothes of so light a grey that they would hardly have been regarded as clerical in a district less remote. He had now reached a goodly age, being full seventy years old; but still he was wiry and active, and showed but few symptoms of decay. His head was bald, and the few remaining locks that surrounded it were nearly white. But there was a look of energy about his mouth, and a humour in his light grey eye, which forbade those who knew him to regard him altogether as an old man. As it was, he could walk from Oxney Colne to Priestown, fifteen long Devonshire miles across the moor; and he who could do that could hardly be regarded as too old for work.

But our present story will have more to do with his daughter than with him. A pretty girl, I have said, was Patience Woolsworthy; and one, too, in many ways remarkable. She had taken her outlook into life, weighing the things which she had and those which she had not, in a manner very unusual, and, as a rule, not always desirable for a young lady. The things which she had not were very many. She had not society; she had not a fortune; she had not any assurance of future means of livelihood; she had not high hope of procuring for herself a position in life by marriage; she had not that excitement and pleasure in life which she read of in such books as found their way down to Oxney Colne Parsonage. It would be easy to add to the list of the things which she had not; and this list against herself she made out with the utmost vigour. The things which she had, or those rather which she assured herself of having, were much more easily counted. She had the birth and education of a lady, the strength of a healthy woman, and a will of her own. Such was the list as she made it out for herself, and I protest that I assert no more than the truth in saying that she never added to it either beauty, wit, or talent.

I began these descriptions by saying that Oxney Colne would, of all places, be the best spot from which a tourist could visit those parts of Devonshire, but for the fact that he could obtain there none of the accommodation which tourists require. A brother antiquarian might, perhaps, in those days have done so, seeing that there was, as I have said, a spare bedroom at the parsonage. Any intimate friend of Miss Le Smyrger's might be as fortunate, for she was equally well provided at Oxney Combe, by which name her house was known. But Miss Le Smyrger was not given to extensive hospitality, and it was only to those who were bound to her, either by ties of blood or of very old friendship, that she delighted to open her doors. As her old friends were very few in number, as those few lived at a distance, and as her nearest relations were higher in the world than she was, and were said by herself to look down upon her, the visits made to Oxney Combe were few and far between.

But now, at the period of which I am writing, such a visit was about to be made. Miss Le Smyrger had a younger sister, who had inherited a property in the parish of Oxney Colne equal to that of the lady who now lived there; but this the younger sister had inherited beauty also, and she therefore, in early life, had found sundry lovers, one of whom became her husband. She had married a man even then well to do in the world, but now rich and almost mighty; a Member of Parliament, a lord of this and that board, a man who had a house in Eaton Square, and a park in the north of England; and in this way her course of life had been very much divided from that of our Miss Le Smyrger. But the Lord of the Government Board had been blessed with various children; and perhaps it was now thought expedient to look after Aunt Penelope's Devonshire acres. Aunt Penelope was empowered to leave them to whom she pleased; and though it was thought in Eaton Square that she must, as a matter of course, leave them to one of the family, nevertheless a little cousinly intercourse might make the thing more certain. I will not say that this was the sole cause of such a visit, but in these days a visit was to be made by Captain Broughton to his aunt. Now Captain John Broughton was the second son of Alfonso Broughton, of Clapham Park and Eaton Square, Member of Parliament, and Lord of the aforesaid Government Board.

"And what do you mean to do with him?" Patience Woolsworthy asked of Miss Le Smyrger when that lady walked over from the Combe to say that her nephew John was to arrive on the following morning.

"Do with him? Why I shall bring him over here to talk to your father."

"He'll be too fashionable for that; and papa won't trouble his head about him if he finds that he doesn't care for Dartmoor."

"Then he may fall in love with you, my dear."

"Well, yes; there's that resource at any rate, and for your sake I dare say I should be more civil to him than papa. But he'll soon get tired of making love, and what you'll do then I cannot imagine."

That Miss Woolsworthy felt no interest in the coming of the Captain I will not pretend to say. The advent of any stranger with whom she would be called on to associate must be matter of interest to her in that secluded place; and she was not so absolutely unlike other young ladies that the arrival of an unmarried young man would be the same to her as the advent of some patriarchal paterfamilias. In taking that outlook into life of which I have spoken, she had never said to herself that she despised those things from which other girls received the excitement, the joys, and the disappointment of their lives. She had simply given herself to understand that very little of such things would come her way, and that it behoved her to live—to live happily if such might be possible—without experiencing the need of them. She had heard, when there was no thought of any such visit to Oxney Colne, that John Broughton was a handsome, clever man—one who thought much of himself, and was thought much of by others—that there had been some talk of his marrying a great heiress, which marriage, however, had not taken place through unwillingness on his part, and that he was on the whole a man of more mark in the world than the ordinary captain of ordinary regiments.

Captain Broughton came to Oxney Combe, stayed there a fortnight,—the intended period for his projected visit having been fixed at three or four days,—and then went his way. He went his way back to his London haunts, the time of the year then being the close of the Easter holidays; but as he did so he told his aunt that he should assuredly return to her in the autumn.

"And assuredly I shall be happy to see you, John—if you come with a certain purpose. If you have no such purpose, you had better remain away."

"I shall assuredly come," the Captain had replied, and then he had gone on his journey.

The summer passed rapidly by, and very little was said between Miss Le Smyrger and Miss Woolsworthy about Captain Broughton. In many respects—nay, I may say, as to all ordinary matters, no two women could well be more intimate with each other than they were,—and more than that, they had the courage each to talk to the other with absolute truth as to things concerning themselves—a courage in which dear friends often fail. But nevertheless, very little was said between them about Captain John Broughton. All that was said may be here repeated.

"John says that he shall return here in August," Miss Le Smyrger said, as Patience was sitting with her in the parlour at Oxney Combe, on the morning after that gentleman's departure.

"He told me so himself," said Patience; and as she spoke her round dark eyes assumed a look of more than ordinary self-will. If Miss Le Smyrger had intended to carry the conversation any further, she changed her mind as she looked at her companion. Then, as I said, the summer ran by, and towards the close of the warm days of July, Miss Le Smyrger, sitting in the same chair in the same room, again took up the conversation.

"I got a letter from John this morning. He says that he shall be here on the third."

"Does he?"

"He is very punctual to the time he named."

"Yes; I fancy that he is a punctual man," said Patience.

"I hope that you will be glad to see him," said Miss Le Smyrger.

"Very glad to see him," said Patience, with a bold clear voice; and then the conversation was again dropped, and nothing further was said till after Captain Broughton's second arrival in the parish.

Four months had then passed since his departure, and during that time Miss Woolsworthy had performed all her usual daily duties in their accustomed course. No one could discover that she had been less careful in her household matters than had been her wont, less willing to go among her poor neighbours, or less assiduous in her attentions to her father. But not the less was there a feeling in the minds of those around her that some great change had come upon her. She would sit during the long summer evenings on a certain spot outside the parsonage orchard, at the top of a small sloping field in which their solitary cow was always pastured, with a book on her knees before her, but rarely reading. There she would sit, with the beautiful view down to the winding river below her, watching the setting sun, and thinking, thinking, thinking—thinking of something of which she had never spoken. Often would Miss Le Smyrger come upon her there, and sometimes would pass by her even without a word; but never—never once did she dare to ask her of the matter of her thoughts. But she knew the matter well enough. No confession was necessary to inform her that Patience Woolsworthy was in love with John Broughton—ay, in love, to the full and entire loss of her whole heart.

On one evening she was so sitting till the July sun had fallen and hidden himself for the night, when her father came upon her as he returned from one of his rambles on the moor. "Patty," he said, "you are always sitting there now. Is it not late? Will you not be cold?"

"No, papa," said she, "I shall not be cold."

"But won't you come to the house? I miss you when you come in so late that there's no time to say a word before we go to bed."

She got up and followed him into the parsonage, and when they were in the sitting-room together, and the door was closed, she came up to him and kissed him.

"Papa," she said, "would it make you very unhappy if I were to leave you?"

"Leave me!" he said, startled by the serious and almost solemn tone of her voice. "Do you mean for always?"

"If I were to marry, papa?"

"Oh, marry! No; that would not make me unhappy. It would make me very happy, Patty, to see you married to a man you would love—very, very happy; though my days would be desolate without you."

"That is it, papa. What would you do if I went from you?"

"What would it matter, Patty? I should be free, at any rate, from a load which often presses heavy on me now. What will you do when I shall leave you? A few more years and all will be over with me. But who is it, love? Has anybody said anything to you?"

"It was only an idea, papa. I don't often think of such a thing; but I did think of it then." And so the subject was allowed to pass by. This had happened before the day of the second arrival had been absolutely fixed and made known to Miss Woolsworthy.

And then that second arrival took place. The reader may have understood from the words with which Miss Le Smyrger authorised her nephew to make his second visit to Oxney Combe that Miss Woolsworthy's passion was not altogether unauthorised. Captain Broughton had been told that he was not to come unless he came with a certain purpose; and having been so told, he still persisted in coming. There can be no doubt but that he well understood the purport to which his aunt alluded. "I shall assuredly come," he had said. And true to his word, he was now there.

Patience knew exactly the hour at which he must arrive at the station at Newton Abbot, and the time also which it would take to travel over those twelve uphill miles from the station to Oxney. It need hardly he said that she paid no visit to Miss Le Smyrger's house on that afternoon; but she might have known something of Captain Broughton's approach without going thither. His road to the Combe passed by the parsonage-gate, and had Patience sat even at her bedroom window she must have seen him. But on such a morning she would not sit at her bedroom window—she would do nothing which would force her to accuse herself of a restless longing for her lover's coming. It was for him to seek her. If he chose to do so, he knew the way to the parsonage.

Miss Le Smyrger—good, dear, honest, hearty Miss Le Smyrger, was in a fever of anxiety on behalf of her friend. It was not that she wished her nephew to marry Patience —or rather that she had entertained any such wish when he first came,—among them. She was not given to match- making, and moreover thought, or had thought within herself, that they of Oxney Colne could do very well without any admixture from Eaton Square. Her plan of life had been that, when old Mr. Woolsworthy was taken away from Dartmoor, Patience should live with her; and that when she also shuffled off her coil, then Patience Woolsworthy should be the maiden mistress of Oxney Combe—of Oxney Combe and Mr. Cloysey's farm— to the utter detriment of all the

Broughtons. Such had been her plan before nephew John had come among them—a plan not to be spoken of till the coming of that dark day which should make Patience an orphan. But now her nephew had been there, and all was to be altered. Miss Le Smyrger's plan would have provided a companion for her old age; but that had not been her chief object. She had thought more of Patience than of herself, and now it seemed that a prospect of a higher happiness was opening for her friend.

"John," she said, as soon as the first greetings were over, "do you remember the last words that I said to you before you went away?" Now, for myself, I much admire Miss Le Smyrger's heartiness, but I do not think much of her discretion. It would have been better, perhaps, had she allowed things to take their course.

"I can't say that I do," said the Captain. At the same time the
Captain did remember very well what those last words had been.

"I am so glad to see you, so delighted to see you, if—if

—if -," and then she paused, for with all her courage she hardly dared to ask her nephew whether he had come there with the express purpose of asking Miss Woolsworthy to marry him.

To tell the truth, for there is no room for mystery within the limits of this short story,—to tell, I say, at a word the plain and simple truth, Captain Broughton had already asked that question. On the day before he left Oxney Come, he had in set terms proposed to the parson's daughter, and indeed the words, the hot and frequent words, which previously to that had fallen like sweetest honey into the ears of Patience Woolsworthy, had made it imperative on him to do so. When a man in such a place as that has talked to a girl of love day after day, must not he talk of it to some definite purpose on the day on which he leaves her? Or if he do not, must he not submit to be regarded as false, selfish, and almost fraudulent? Captain Broughton, however, had asked the question honestly and truly. He had done so honestly and truly, but in words, or, perhaps, simply with a tone, that had hardly sufficed to satisfy the proud spirit of the girl he loved. She by that time had confessed to herself that she loved him with all her heart; but she had made no such confession to him. To him she had spoken no word, granted no favour, that any lover might rightfully regard as a token of love returned. She had listened to him as he spoke, and bade him keep such sayings for the drawing-rooms of his fashionable friends. Then he had spoken out and had asked for that hand,—not, perhaps, as a suitor tremulous with hope,—but as a rich man who knows that he can command that which he desires to purchase.

"You should think more of this," she had said to him at last. "If you would really have me for your wife, it will not be much to you to return here again when time for thinking of it shall have passed by." With these words she had dismissed him, and now he had again come back to Oxney Colne. But still she would not place herself at the window to look for him, nor dress herself in other than her simple morning country dress, nor omit one item of her daily work. If he wished to take her at all, he should wish to take her as she really was, in her plain country life, but he should take her also with full observance of all those privileges which maidens are allowed to claim from their lovers. He should contract no ceremonious observance because she was the daughter of a poor country parson who would come to him without a shilling, whereas he stood high in the world's books. He had asked her to give him all that she had, and that all she was ready to give, without stint. But the gift must be valued before it could be given or received, he also was to give her as much, and she would accept it as beyond all price. But she would not allow that that which was offered to her was in any degree the more precious because of his outward worldly standing.

She would not pretend to herself that she thought he would come to her that day, and therefore she busied herself in the kitchen and about the house, giving directions to her two maids as though the afternoon would pass as all other days did pass in that household.

They usually dined at four, and she rarely in these summer months went far from the house before that hour. At four precisely she sat down with her father, and then said that she was going up as far as Helpholme after dinner. Helpholme was a solitary farmhouse in another parish, on the border of the moor, and Mr. Woolsworthy asked her whether he should accompany her.

"Do, papa," she said, "if you are not too tired." And yet she had thought how probable it might be that she should meet John Broughton on her walk. And so it was arranged; but just as dinner was over, Mr. Woolsworthy remembered himself.

"Gracious me," he said, "how my memory is going. Gribbles, from Ivybridge, and old John Poulter, from Bovey, are coming to meet here by appointment. You can't put Helpholme off till to-morrow?"

Patience, however, never put off anything, and therefore at six o'clock, when her father had finished his slender modicum of toddy, she tied on her hat and went on her walk. She started with a quick step, and left no word to say by which route she would go. As she passed up along the little lane which led towards Oxney Combe, she would not even look to see if he was coming towards her; and when she left the road, passing over a stone stile into a little path which ran first through the upland fields, and then across the moor ground towards Helpholme, she did not look back once, or listen for his coming step.

She paid her visit, remaining upwards of an hour with the old bedridden mother of the tenant of Helpholme. "God bless you, my darling!" said the old woman as she left her; "and send you some one to make your own path bright and happy through the world." These words were still ringing in her ears with all their significance as she saw John Broughton waiting for her at the first stile which she had to pass after leaving the farmer's haggard.

"Patty," he said, as he took her hand, and held it close within both his own, "what a chase I have had after you!"

"And who asked you, Captain Broughton?" she answered, smiling. "If the journey was too much for your poor London strength, could you not have waited till to-morrow morning, when you would have found me at the parsonage?" But she did not draw her hand away from him, or in any way pretend that he had not a right to accost her as a lover.

"No, I could not wait. I am more eager to see those I love than you seem to be."

"How do you know whom I love, or how eager I might be to see them? There is an old woman there whom I love, and I have thought nothing of this walk with the object of seeing her." And now, slowly drawing her hand away from him, she pointed to the farmhouse which she had left.

"Patty," he said, after a minute's pause, during which she had looked full into his face with all the force of her bright eyes; "I have come from London to-day, straight down here to Oxney, and from my aunt's house close upon your footsteps after you, to ask you that one question—Do you love me?"

"What a Hercules!" she said, again laughing. "Do you

really mean that you left London only this morning? Why, you must have been five hours in a railway carriage and two in a postchaise, not to talk of the walk afterwards. You ought to take more care of yourself, Captain Broughton!"

He would have been angry with her—for he did not like to be quizzed— had she not put her hand on his arm as she spoke, and the softness of her touch had redeemed the offence of her words.

"All that I have done," said he, "that I may hear one word from you."

"That any word of mine should have such potency! But let us walk on, or my father will take us for some of the standing stones of the moor. How have you found your aunt? If you only knew the cares that have sat on her dear shoulders for the last week past, in order that your high mightiness might have a sufficiency to eat and drink in these desolate half-starved regions!"

"She might have saved herself such anxiety. No one can care less for such things than I do."

"And yet I think I have heard you boast of the cook of your club." And then again there was silence for a minute or two.

"Patty," said he, stopping again in the path; "answer my question. I have a right to demand an answer. Do you love me?"

"And what if I do? What if I have been so silly as to allow your perfections to be too many for my weak heart? What then, Captain Broughton?"

"It cannot be that you love me, or you would not joke now."

"Perhaps not, indeed," she said. It seemed as though she were resolved not to yield an inch in her own humour. And then again they walked on.

"Patty," he said once more, "I shall get an answer from you to-night,— this evening; now, during this walk, or I shall return to-morrow, and never revisit this spot again."

"Oh, Captain Broughton, how should we ever manage to live without you?"

"Very well," he said; "up to the end of this walk I can

hear it all;— and one word spoken then will mend it all."

During the whole of this time she felt that she was ill-using him. She knew that she loved him with all her heart; that it would nearly kill her to part with him; that she had heard his renewed offer with an ecstacy of joy. She acknowledged to herself that he was giving proof of his devotion as strong as any which a girl could receive from her lover. And yet she could hardly bring herself to say the word he longed to hear. That word once said, and then she knew that she must succumb to her love for ever! That word once said, and there would be nothing for her but to spoil him with her idolatry! That word once said, and she must continue to repeat it into his ears, till perhaps he might be tired of hearing it! And now he had threatened her, and how could she speak after that? She certainly would not speak it unless he asked her again without such threat. And so they walked on in silence.

"Patty," he said at last. "By the heavens above us you shall answer me. Do you love me?"

She now stood still, and almost trembled as she looked up into his face. She stood opposite to him for a moment, and then placing her two hands on his shoulders, she answered him. "I do, I do, I do," she said, "with all my heart; with all my heart—with all my heart and strength." And then her head fell upon his breast.

* * *

Captain Broughton was almost as much surprised as delighted by the warmth of the acknowledgment made by the eager-hearted passionate girl whom he now held within his arms. She had said it now; the words had been spoken; and there was nothing for her but to swear to him over and over again with her sweetest oaths, that those words were true—true as her soul. And very sweet was the walk down from thence to the parsonage gate. He spoke no more of the distance of the ground, or the length of his day's journey. But he stopped her at every turn that he might press her arm the closer to his own, that he might look into the brightness of her eyes, and prolong his hour of delight. There were no more gibes now on her tongue, no raillery at his London finery, no laughing comments on his coming and going. With downright honesty she told him everything: how she had loved him before her heart was warranted in such a passion; how, with much thinking, she had resolved that it would be unwise to take him at his first word, and had thought it better that he should return to London, and then think over it; how she had almost repented of her courage when she had feared, during those long summer days, that he would forget her; and how her heart had leapt for joy when her old friend had told her that he was coming.

"And yet," said he, "you were not glad to see me!"

"Oh, was I not glad? You cannot understand the feelings of a girl who has lived secluded as I have done. Glad is no word for the joy I felt. But it was not seeing you that I cared for so much. It was the knowledge that you were near me once again. I almost wish now that I had not seen you till to-morrow." But as she spoke she pressed his arm, and this caress gave the lie to her last words.

"No, do not come in to-night," she said, when she reached the little wicket that led up to the parsonage. "Indeed, you shall not. I could not behave myself properly if you did."

"But I don't want you to behave properly."

"Oh! I am to keep that for London, am I? But, nevertheless, Captain
Broughton, I will not invite you either to tea or to supper to-night."

"Surely I may shake hands with your father."

"Not to-night—not till—John, I may tell him, may I not? I must tell him at once."

"Certainly," said he.

"And then you shall see him to-morrow. Let me see— at what hour shall
I bid you come?"

"To breakfast."

"No, indeed. What on earth would your aunt do with her broiled turkey and the cold pie? I have got no cold pie for you."

"I hate cold pie."

"What a pity! But, John, I should be forced to leave you directly after breakfast. Come down—come down at two, or three; and then I will go back with you to Aunt Penelope. I must see her to-morrow;" and so at last the matter was settled, and the happy Captain, as he left her, was hardly resisted in his attempt to press her lips to his own.

When she entered the parlour in which her father was sitting, there still were Gribbles and Poulter discussing some knotty point of Devon lore. So Patience took off her hat, and sat herself down, waiting till they should go. For full an hour she had to wait, and then Gribbles and Poulter did go. But it was not in such matters as this that Patience Woolsworthy was impatient. She could wait, and wait, and wait, curbing herself for weeks and months, while the thing waited for was in her eyes good; but she could not curb her hot thoughts or her hot words when things came to be discussed which she did not think to be good.

"Papa," she said, when Gribbles' long-drawn last word had been spoken at the door. "Do you remember how I asked you the other day what you would say if I were to leave you?"

"Yes, surely," he replied, looking up at her in astonishment.

"I am going to leave you now," she said. "Dear, dearest father, how am
I to go from you?"

"Going to leave me," said he, thinking of her visit to Helpholme, and thinking of nothing else.

Now, there had been a story about Helpholme. That bedridden old lady there had a stalwart son, who was now the owner of the Helpholme pastures. But though owner in fee of all those wild acres, and of the cattle which they supported, he was not much above the farmers around him, either in manners or education. He had his merits, however; for he was honest, well-to-do in the world, and modest withal. How strong love had grown up, springing from neighbourly kindness, between our Patience and his mother, it needs not here to tell; but rising from it had come another love—or an ambition which might have grown to love. The young man, after much thought, had not dared to speak to Miss Woolsworthy, but he had sent a message by Miss Le Smyrger. If there could be any hope for him, he would present himself as a suitor—on trial. He did not owe a shilling in the world, and had money by him— saved. He wouldn't ask the parson for a shilling of fortune. Such had been the tenor of his message, and Miss Le Smyrger had delivered it faithfully. "He does not mean it," Patience had said with her stern voice. "Indeed he does, my dear. You may be sure he is in earnest," Miss Le Smyrger had replied; "and there is not an honester man in these parts."

"Tell him," said Patience, not attending to the latter portion of her friend's last speech, "that it cannot be— make him understand, you know—and tell him also that the matter shall be thought of no more." The matter had, at any rate, been spoken of no more, but the young farmer still remained a bachelor, and Helpholme still wanted a mistress. But all this came back upon the parson's mind when his daughter told him that she was about to leave him.

"Yes, dearest," she said; and as she spoke she now knelt at his knees.

"I have been asked in marriage, and I have given myself away."

"Well, my love, if you will be happy—"

"I hope I shall; I think I shall. But you, papa?"

"You will not be far from us."

"Oh, yes; in London."

"In London?"

"Captain Broughton lives in London generally."

"And has Captain Broughton asked you to marry him?"

"Yes, papa—who else? Is he not good? Will you not love him? Oh, papa, do not say that I am wrong to love him?"

He never told her his mistake, or explained to her that he had not thought it possible that the high-placed son of the London great man should have fallen in love with his undowered daughter; but he embraced her, and told her, with all his enthusiasm, that he rejoiced in her joy, and would be happy in her happiness. "My own Patty," he said, "I have ever known that you were too good for this life of ours here." And then the evening wore away into the night, with many tears, but still with much happiness.

Captain Broughton, as he walked back to Oxney Combe, made up his mind that he would say nothing on the matter to his aunt till the next morning. He wanted to think over it all, and to think it over, if possible, by himself. He had taken a step in life, the most important that a man is ever called on to take, and he had to reflect whether or no he had taken it with wisdom.

"Have you seen her?" said Miss Le Smyrger, very anxiously, when he came into the drawing-room.

"Miss Woolsworthy you mean," said he. "Yes, I've seen

her. As I found her out, I took a long walk, and happened to meet her. Do you know, aunt, I think I'll go to bed; I was up at five this morning, and have been on the move ever since."

Miss Le Smyrger perceived that she was to hear nothing that evening, so she handed him his candlestick and allowed him to go to his room.

But Captain Broughton did not immediately retire to bed, nor when he did so was he able to sleep at once. Had this step that he had taken been a wise one? He was not a man who, in worldly matters, had allowed things to arrange themselves for him, as is the case with so many men. He had formed views for himself, and had a theory of life. Money for money's sake he had declared to himself to be bad. Money, as a concomitant to things which were in themselves good, he had declared to himself to be good also. That concomitant in this affair of his marriage, he had now missed. Well; he had made up his mind to that, and would put up with the loss. He had means of living of his own, the means not so extensive as might have been desirable. That it would be well for him to become a married man, looking merely to the state of life as opposed to his present state, he had fully resolved. On that point, therefore, there was nothing to repent. That Patty Woolsworthy was good, affectionate, clever, and beautiful, he was sufficiently satisfied. It would be odd indeed if he were not so satisfied now, seeing that for the last four months he had so declared to himself daily with many inward asseverations. And yet though he repeated, now again, that he was satisfied, I do not think that he was so fully satisfied of it as he had been throughout the whole of those four months. It is sad to say so, but I fear—I fear that such was the case. When you have your plaything, how much of the anticipated pleasure vanishes, especially if it be won easily.

He had told none of his family what were his intentions in this second visit to Devonshire, and now he had to bethink himself whether they would be satisfied. What would his sister say, she who had married the

Honourable Augustus Gumbleton, gold-stick-in-waiting to Her Majesty's Privy Council? Would she receive Patience with open arms, and make much of her about London? And then how far would London suit Patience, or would Patience suit London? There would be much for him to do in teaching her, and it would be well for him to set about the lesson without loss of time. So far he got that night, but when the morning came he went a step further, and began mentally to criticise her manner to himself. It had been very sweet, that warm, that full, that ready declaration of love. Yes; it had been very sweet; but—but—; when, after her little jokes, she did confess her love, had she not been a little too free for feminine excellence? A man likes to be told that he is loved, but he hardly wishes that the girl he is to marry should fling herself at his head!

Ah me! yes; it was thus he argued to himself as on that morning he went through the arrangements of his toilet. "Then he was a brute," you say, my pretty reader. I have never said that he was not a brute. But this I remark, that many such brutes are to be met with in the beaten paths of the world's highway. When Patience Woolsworthy had answered him coldly, bidding him go back to London and think over his love; while it seemed from her manner that at any rate as yet she did not care for him; while he was absent from her, and, therefore, longing for her, the possession of her charms, her talent and bright honesty of purpose had seemed to him a thing most desirable. Now they were his own. They had, in fact, been his own from the first. The heart of this country-bred girl had fallen at the first word from his mouth. Had she not so confessed to him? She was very nice— very nice indeed. He loved her dearly. But had he not sold himself too cheaply?

I by no means say that he was not a brute. But whether brute or no, he was an honest man, and had no remotest dream, either then, on that morning, or during the following days on which such thoughts pressed more quickly on his mind—of breaking away from his pledged word. At breakfast on that morning he told all to Miss Le

Smyrger, and that lady, with warm and gracious intentions, confided to him her purpose regarding her property. "I have always regarded Patience as my heir," she said, "and shall do so still."

"Oh, indeed," said Captain Broughton.

"But it is a great, great pleasure to me to think that she will give back the little property to my sister's child. You will have your mother's, and thus it will all come together again."

"Ah!" said Captain Broughton. He had his own ideas about property, and did not, even under existing circumstances, like to hear that his aunt considered herself at liberty to leave the acres away to one who was by blood quite a stranger to the family.

"Does Patience know of this?" he asked.

"Not a word," said Miss Le Smyrger. And then nothing more was said upon the subject.

On that afternoon he went down and received the parson's benediction and congratulations with a good grace. Patience said very little on the occasion, and indeed was absent during the greater part of the interview. The two lovers then walked up to Oxney Combe, and there were more benedictions and more congratulations. "All went merry as a marriage bell," at any rate as far as Patience was concerned. Not a word had yet fallen from that dear mouth, not a look had yet come over that handsome face, which tended in any way to mar her bliss. Her first day of acknowledged love was a day altogether happy, and when she prayed for him as she knelt beside her bed there was no feeling in her mind that any fear need disturb her joy.

I will pass over the next three or four days very quickly, merely saying that Patience did not find them so pleasant as that first day after her engagement. There was something in her lover's manner— something which at first she could not define—which by degrees seemed to grate against her feelings.

He was sufficiently affectionate, that being a matter on which she did not require much demonstration; but joined to his affection there seemed to be—; she hardly liked to suggest to herself a harsh word, but could it be possible that he was beginning to think that she was not good enough for him? And then she asked herself the question—was she good enough for him? If there were doubt about that, the match should be broken off, though she tore her own heart out in the struggle. The truth, however, was this—that he had begun that teaching which he had already found to be so necessary. Now, had any one essayed to teach Patience German or mathematics, with that young lady's free consent, I believe that she would have been found a meek scholar. But it was not probable that she would be meek when she found a self-appointed tutor teaching her manners and conduct without her consent.

So matters went on for four or five days, and on the evening of the fifth day Captain Broughton and his aunt drank tea at the parsonage. Nothing very especial occurred; but as the parson and Miss La Smyrger insisted on playing backgammon with devoted perseverance during the whole evening, Broughton had a good opportunity of saying a word or two about those changes in his lady-love which a life in London would require—and some word he said also—some single slight word as to the higher station in life to which he would exalt his bride. Patience bore it—for her father and Miss La Smyrger were in the room—she bore it well, speaking no syllable of anger, and enduring, for the moment, the implied scorn of the old parsonage. Then the evening broke up, and Captain Broughton walked back to Oxney Combe with his aunt. "Patty," her father said to her before they went to bed, "he seems to me to be a most excellent young man." "Dear papa," she answered, kissing him. "And terribly deep in love," said Mr. Woolsworthy. "Oh, I don't know about that," she answered, as she left him with her sweetest smile. But though she could thus smile at her father's joke, she had already made up her mind that there was still something to be learned as to her promised husband before she could place herself altogether in his hands. She would ask him whether he thought himself liable to injury from this proposed marriage; and though he should deny any such thought, she would know from the manner of his denial what his true feelings were.

And he, too, on that night, during his silent walk with Miss Le Smyrger, had entertained some similar thoughts. "I fear she is obstinate," he said to himself; and then he had half accused her of being sullen also. "If that be her temper, what a life of misery I have before me!"

"Have you fixed a day yet?" his aunt asked him as they came near to her house.

"No, not yet; I don't know whether it will suit me to fix it before I leave."

"Why, it was but the other day you were in such a hurry."

"Ah—yes—I have thought more about it since then."

"I should have imagined that this would depend on what Patty thinks," said Miss Le Smyrger, standing up for the privileges of her sex. "It is presumed that the gentleman is always ready as soon as the lady will consent."

"Yes, in ordinary cases it is so; but when a girl is taken out of her own sphere—"

"Her own sphere! Let me caution you, Master John, not to talk to Patty about her own sphere."

"Aunt Penelope, as Patience is to be my wife and not yours, I must claim permission to speak to her on such subjects as may seem suitable to me." And then they parted—not in the best humour with each other.

On the following day Captain Broughton and Miss Woolsworthy did not meet till the evening. She had said, before those few ill-omened words had passed her lover's lips, that she would probably be at Miss Le Smyrger's house on the following morning. Those ill-omened words did pass her lover's lips, and then she remained at home. This did not come from sullenness, nor even from anger, but from a conviction that it would be well that she should think much before she met him again. Nor was he anxious to hurry a meeting. His thought—his base thought— was this; that she would be sure to come up to the Combe after him; but she did not come, and therefore in the evening he went down to her, and asked her to walk with him.

They went away by the path that led to Helpholme, and little was said between them till they had walked some mile together.

Patience, as she went along the path, remembered almost to the letter the sweet words which had greeted her ears as she came down that way with him on the night of his arrival; but he remembered nothing of that sweetness then. Had he not made an ass of himself during these last six months? That was the thought which very much had possession of his mind.

"Patience," he said at last, having hitherto spoken only an indifferent word now and again since they had left the parsonage, "Patience, I hope you realise the importance of the step which you and I are about to take?"

"Of course I do," she answered. "What an odd question that is for you to ask!"

"Because," said he, "sometimes I almost doubt it. It seems to me as though you thought you could remove yourself from here to your new home with no more trouble than when you go from home up to the Combe."

"Is that meant for a reproach, John?"

"No, not for a reproach, but for advice. Certainly not for a reproach."

"I am glad of that."

"But I should wish to make you think how great is the leap in the world which you are about to take." Then again they walked on for many steps before she answered him.

"Tell me, then, John," she said, when she had sufficiently considered what words she should speak; and as she spoke a bright colour suffused her face, and her eyes flashed almost with anger. "What leap do you mean? Do you mean a leap upwards?"

"Well, yes; I hope it will be so."

"In one sense, certainly, it would be a leap upwards. To be the wife of the man I loved; to have the privilege of holding his happiness in my hand; to know that I was his own—the companion whom he had chosen out of all the world—that would, indeed, be a leap upwards; a leap almost to heaven, if all that were so. But if you mean upwards in any other sense—"

"I was thinking of the social scale."

"Then, Captain Broughton, your thoughts were doing me dishonour."

"Doing you dishonour!"

"Yes, doing me dishonour. That your father is, in the world's esteem, a greater man than mine is doubtless true enough. That you, as a man, are richer than I am as a woman, is doubtless also true. But you dishonour me, and yourself also, if these things can weigh with you now."

"Patience,—I think you can hardly know what words you are saying to me."

"Pardon me, but I think I do. Nothing that you can give me—no gifts of that description—can weigh aught against that which I am giving you. If you had all the wealth and rank of the greatest lord in the land, it would count as nothing in such a scale. If—as I have not doubted—if in return for my heart you have given me yours, then—then--then you have paid me fully. But when gifts such as those are going, nothing else can count even as a make-weight."

"I do not quite understand you," he answered, after a pause. "I fear you are a little high-flown." And then, while the evening was still early, they walked back to the parsonage almost without another word.

Captain Broughton at this time had only one full day more to remain at Oxney Colne. On the afternoon following that he was to go as far as Exeter, and thence return to London. Of course, it was to be expected that the wedding day would be fixed before he went, and much had been said about it during the first day or two of his engagement. Then he had pressed for an early time, and Patience, with a girl's usual diffidence, had asked for some little delay. But now nothing was said on the subject; and how was it probable that such a matter could be settled after such a conversation as that which I have related? That evening, Miss Le Smyrger asked whether the day had been fixed. "No," said Captain Broughton, harshly; "nothing has been fixed." "But it will be arranged before you go?" "Probably not," he said; and then the subject was dropped for the time.

"John," she said, just before she went to bed, "if there be anything wrong between you and Patience, I conjure you to tell me."

"You had better ask her," he replied. "I can tell you nothing."

On the following morning he was much surprised by seeing Patience on the gravel path before Miss Le Smyrger's gate immediately after breakfast. He went to the door to open it for her, and she, as she gave him her hand, told him that she came up to speak to him. There was no hesitation in her manner, nor any look of anger in her face. But there was in her gait and form, in her voice and countenance, a fixedness of purpose which he had never seen before, or at any rate had never acknowledged.

"Certainly," said he. "Shall I come out with you, or will you come up stairs?"

"We can sit down in the summer-house," she said; and thither they both went.

"Captain Broughton," she said—and she began her task the moment that they were both seated—"you and I have engaged ourselves as man and wife, but perhaps we have been over rash."

"How so?" said he.

"It may be—and indeed I will say more—it is the case that we have made this engagement without knowing enough of each other's character."

"I have not thought so."

"The time will perhaps come when you will so think, but for the sake of all that we most value, let it come before it is too late. What would be our fate—how terrible would be our misery—if such a thought should come to either of us after we have linked our lots together."

There was a solemnity about her as she thus spoke which almost repressed him,—which for a time did prevent him from taking that tone of authority which on such a subject he would choose to adopt. But he recovered himself. "I hardly think that this comes well from you," he said.

"From whom else should it come? Who else can fight my battle for me; and, John, who else can fight that same battle on your behalf? I tell you this, that with your mind standing towards me as it does stand at present, you could not give me your hand at the altar with true words and a happy conscience. Am I not true? You have half repented of your bargain already. Is it not so?"

He did not answer her; but getting up from his seat walked to the front of the summer-house, and stood there with his back turned upon her. It was not that he meant to be ungracious, but in truth he did not know how to answer her. He had half repented of his bargain.

"John," she said, getting up and following him, so that she could put her hand upon his arm, "I have been very angry with you."

"Angry with me!" he said, turning sharp upon her.

"Yes, angry with you. You would have treated me like

a child. But that feeling has gone now. I am not angry now. There is my hand;—the hand of a friend. Let the words that have been spoken between us be as though they had not been spoken. Let us both be free."

"Do you mean it?"

"Certainly I mean it." As she spoke these words her eyes filled with tears, in spite of all the efforts she could make; but he was not looking at her, and her efforts had sufficed to prevent any sob from being audible.

"With all my heart," he said; and it was manifest from his tone that he had no thought of her happiness as he spoke. It was true that she had been angry with him—angry, as she had herself declared; but nevertheless, in what she had said and what she had done, she had thought more of his happiness than of her own. Now she was angry once again.

"With all your heart, Captain Broughton! Well, so be it. If with all your heart, then is the necessity so much the greater. You go to- morrow. Shall we say farewell now?"

"Patience, I am not going to be lectured."

"Certainly not by me. Shall we say farewell now?"

"Yes, if you are determined."

"I am determined. Farewell, Captain Broughton. You have all my wishes for your happiness." And she held out her hand to him.

"Patience!" he said. And he looked at her with a dark frown, as though he would strive to frighten her into submission. If so, he might have saved himself any such attempt.

"Farewell, Captain Broughton. Give me your hand, for I cannot stay." He gave her his hand, hardly knowing why he did so. She lifted it to her lips and kissed it, and then, leaving him, passed from the summer- house down through the wicket-gate, and straight home to the parsonage.

During the whole of that day she said no word to any one of what had occurred. When she was once more at home she went about her household affairs as she had done on that day of his arrival. When she sat down to dinner with her father he observed nothing to make him think that she was unhappy; nor during the evening was there any expression in her face, or any tone in her voice, which excited his attention. On the following morning Captain Broughton called at the parsonage, and the servant-girl brought word to her mistress that he was in the parlour. But she would not see him. "Laws, miss, you ain't a quarrelled with your beau?" the poor girl said. "No, not quarrelled," she said; "but give him that." It was a scrap of paper, containing a word or two in pencil. "It is better that we should not meet again. God bless you." And from that day to this, now more than ten years, they never have met.

"Papa," she said to her father that afternoon, "dear papa, do not be angry with me. It is all over between me and John Broughton. Dearest, you and I will not be separated." It would be useless here to tell how great was the old man's surprise and how true his sorrow. As the tale was told to him no cause was given for anger with any one. Not a word was spoken against the suitor who had on that day returned to London with a full conviction that now at least he was relieved from his engagement. "Patty, my darling child," he said, "may God grant that it be for the best!

"It is for the best," she answered stoutly. "For this place I am fit; and I much doubt whether I am fit for any other."

On that day she did not see Miss Le Smyrger, but on the following morning, knowing that Captain Broughton had gone off, having heard the wheels of the carriage as they passed by the parsonage gate on his way to the station,—she walked up to the Combe.

"He has told you, I suppose?" said she.

"Yes," said Miss Le Smyrger. "And I will never see him again unless he asks your pardon on his knees. I have told him so. I would not even give him my hand as he went."

"But why so, thou kindest one? The fault was mine more than his."

"I understand. I have eyes in my head," said the old maid. "I have watched him for the last four or five days. If you could have kept the truth to yourself and bade him keep off from you, he would have been at your feet now, licking the dust from your shoes."

"But, dear friend, I do not want a man to lick dust from my shoes."

"Ah, you are a fool. You do not know the value of your own wealth."

"True; I have been a fool. I was a fool to think that one coming from such a life as he has led could be happy with such as I am. I know the truth now. I have bought the lesson dearly,—but perhaps not too dearly, seeing that it will never be forgotten."

There was but little more said about the matter between our three friends at Oxney Colne. What, indeed, could be said? Miss Le Smyrger for a year or two still expected that her nephew would return and claim his bride; but he has never done so, nor has there been any correspondence between them. Patience Woolsworthy had learned her lesson dearly. She had given her whole heart to the man; and, though she so bore herself that no one was aware of the violence of the struggle, nevertheless the struggle within her bosom was very violent. She never told herself that she had done wrong; she never regretted her loss; but yet—yet—the loss was very hard to bear. He also had loved her, but he was not capable of a love which could much injure his daily peace. Her daily peace was gone for many a day to come.

Her father is still living; but there is a curate now in the parish. In conjunction with him and with Miss Le Smyrger she spends her time in the concerns of the parish. In her own eyes she is a confirmed old maid; and such is my opinion also. The romance of her life was played out in that summer. She never sits now lonely on the hill-side thinking how much she might do for one whom she really loved. But with a large heart she loves many, and, with no romance, she works hard to lighten the burdens of those she loves.

As for Captain Broughton, all the world know that he did marry that great heiress with whom his name was once before connected, and that he is now a useful member of Parliament, working on committees three or four days a week with a zeal that is indefatigable. Sometimes, not often, as he thinks of Patience Woolsworthy, a gratified smile comes across his face.

Printed in Great Britain
by Amazon

22669309R00036